TORGOR
THE
MINOTAUR

BY ADAM BLADE

ORCHARD

WELL

CITY
GATES

MALVEL'S
CASTLE

THE WESTERN CITY

THE RIVER

GATEWAY TO
AVANTIA

MARSHES

WELCOME TO

Collect the special coins in this book.
You will earn one gold coin for
every chapter you read.

Once you have finished all the chapters,
find out what to do with your gold coins at
the back of the book.

With special thanks to Cherith Baldry

For Cameron and Brandon, true heroes

www.beastquest.co.uk

ORCHARD BOOKS
Carmelite House
50 Victoria Embankment
London EC4Y 0DZ

A Paperback Original
First published in Great Britain in 2008
This edition published in 2015

Beast Quest is a registered trademark of Beast Quest Limited
Series created by Beast Quest Limited, London

Text © Beast Quest Limited 2008
Cover and inside illustrations by Steve Sims © Beast Quest Limited
2008

A CIP catalogue record for this book is available from
the British Library.

ISBN 978 1 40834 775 1

1 3 5 7 9 10 8 6 4 2

Printed in Great Britain by Clays Ltd, St Ives plc

	MIX
FSC www.fsc.org	Paper from responsible sources FSC® C104740

The paper and board used in this book are made from wood
from responsible sources.

Orchard Books
An imprint of Hachette Children's Group
Part of The Watts Publishing Group Limited
An Hachette UK Company

www.hachette.co.uk

Gorgonia

DENSE FOREST

REBEL SETTLEMENT OF KALOOM

RAINFOREST

VALLEYS

RUINED CASTLE

THE BLACK OCEAN

CONTENTS

Welcome. You stand on the edge of darkness, at the gates of an awful land. This place is Gorgonia, the Dark Realm, where the sky is red, the water black and Malvel rules. Tom and Elenna – your hero and his companion – must travel here to complete the next Beast Quest.

Gorgonia is home to six of the deadliest Beasts imaginable – minotaur, winged stallion, sea monster, Gorgon hound, mighty mammoth and scorpion man. Nothing can prepare Tom and Elenna for what they are about to face. Their past victories mean nothing. Only strong hearts and determination will save them now.

Dare you follow Tom's path once more? I advise you to turn back. Heroes can be stubborn and adventures may beckon, but if you decide to stay with Tom, you must be brave and fearless. Anything less will mean certain doom.

Watch where you step…

Kerlo the Gatekeeper

PROLOGUE

Hector's heart pounded as he ran through the forest. He had spent too long playing by the stream and now the moon was rising, purple and threatening. The angry red sky of Gorgonia swirled above his head. As he wove through the trees, the shadows seemed alive with danger.

Hector paused in a clearing to catch his breath, and tried to see if any evil forest creatures lurked nearby. His heart beat faster as he heard a rustling sound. He darted behind a tree and pressed himself against the trunk.

Peering out, he spotted two young men crawling towards him. They kept glancing back fearfully, as if they were being followed. Hector gasped as he saw the silver talismans around their necks. These were only worn by the Gorgonian rebels, who lived in the woods and plotted to overthrow the Dark Wizard, Malvel. Hector's father had told him that they were wasting their time. Malvel had long ruled Gorgonia – that would never change.

The two young men crept
across the clearing and disguised
themselves behind a tangle of
ivy. They were now completely
concealed. Still Hector did not
dare come out from behind the
tree. What were these two young
men hiding from? Was Malvel on
their trail? Hector felt his mouth
go dry. What if the evil wizard
found him cowering here, alone
in the forest? Malvel would think
that he was in league with the
rebels!

The ground suddenly trembled
beneath his feet. Hector looked
up to see a huge figure striding
through the trees towards him,
an enormous axe in its hand.

The purple moonlight glinted off the golden blade as the fearsome creature swung the axe over its head, slashing through the trees that stood in the way. Hector tried to move but fear had made his limbs useless.

A sob of terror escaped his throat. He had never seen this creature before, but he knew who it was: Torgor the Minotaur, one of the six Evil Beasts of Gorgonia and loyal servant to Malvel.

The minotaur halted, looking down, and spotted Hector. His eyes narrowed. He was as towering as the forest trees, and his vast body was covered with a thick, glistening pelt of coal-black

hair. Two twisted horns rose from either side of his bull-like head. His arms swelled with muscles and one huge fist was clasped around the axe's handle. The Beast tested the sharp edge of the weapon's blade with his thumb.

"Don't hurt me," Hector begged. He felt faint at the thought of the axe swishing through the air towards him. The blade would cut off his head with one blow.

The Beast let out a threatening snarl and saliva dripped from his jaws. Then he raised the axe above Hector's head.

"No, wait!" Hector shouted. He knew Malvel must have sent the Beast to hunt down the rebels, and had an idea of how he could save himself. "I'm not the one you're looking for." He pointed, with a trembling hand, to the ivy thicket where the two men were hiding. "Look over there." Hot shame flooded through him, but his only thought was getting away from the fearsome Beast and the deadly axe.

Torgor strode across the clearing. With one swish of his axe he slashed the ivy into shreds, revealing the two rebels. They sprang up with cries of terror. For a moment their eyes locked with Hector's and then they bolted deeper into the forest. The minotaur let out a furious roar and raced after them.

Hector sank to the ground, trembling. At last, the thud of the Beast's footsteps died away. Only then did he dare to get up and head in the opposite direction, towards his home.

His legs shook and he stumbled over tree roots as he struggled to the edge of the forest. He knew he had condemned two men to certain death.

"But I'm still alive," he whispered to himself.

1

THROUGH THE LION'S GATE

The air tingled as Tom stepped into the lion's gate. It had appeared from the lake in Avantia after he had defeated Trillion, the evil three-headed lion, but Tom had no idea what lay on the other side.

His horse, Storm, reared up. "Steady, boy," Tom murmured, patting the stallion's glossy neck.

Storm rolled his eyes nervously, but let Tom lead him forwards.

Tom's friend Elenna walked at his other side, with Silver close by. The grey wolf raised his muzzle and whined mournfully.

"We have to do this," Tom muttered through clenched teeth. "Malvel is here somewhere, I know it!"

"You're right, Tom." Elenna's voice was steady. "And we have to rescue Aduro."

Tom stepped out of the gate. A flash of pure white light almost blinded him and a shudder of energy shot through his body. He stumbled and had to hold onto Storm's reins to keep himself from falling. He heard Elenna cry out in shock and Silver give a high-pitched howl.

When Tom's eyes cleared once more he found himself standing in a wasteland. Flat, featureless ground stretched out as far as he could see. A few plants with limp, dark leaves and sprawling stems poked up through the gritty soil, looking as if they were dead or dying. A gnarled tree, bare of leaves, stretched out its twisted branches towards the four friends, and grey cloud hung low beneath a red, swirling sky. In the other direction lay desolate marshes, with reed beds and scum-filled pools. Huge bubbles rose to the surface of the filthy water, and burst with a gurgle and a foul smell.

"Ugh!" Elenna choked out. "The whole place reeks. Has Malvel poisoned everything?"

Tom shivered and set his teeth against the damp, cold air, while Elenna pulled her shawl out of Storm's saddlebag and drew it tightly around her shoulders. "What place is this?" she asked.

"It is the kingdom of Gorgonia," a stranger's voice said from behind them.

They spun round to see a tall figure, dressed in ragged brown robes, standing just in front of the lion's gate. Tom reached for his

sword. Silver let out a growl from deep inside his throat, and Elenna grasped her bow, taking an arrow from her quiver.

The newcomer leant on a staff

of gnarled wood, staring at them.
His head was bald. One eye was
covered by an eye-patch, the other
was a glittering grey.

"Who are you?" Tom asked boldly.
He gripped his sword more tightly
as the man shuffled forwards.
"Don't come any closer."

The strange man's mouth twisted
in amusement. "Have I threatened
you?" He gave a bow. "My name
is Kerlo. I am the gatekeeper of
Gorgonia."

"Are you a servant to Malvel?"
Tom demanded.

"I am not," Kerlo said. "I do not
serve any king or wizard. I simply
watch the gate."

Tom wasn't sure he could trust

this man, but there was no one else to ask for information. "What do you know about Malvel?" he said. "I have to find him. Does he live near here?"

Again Kerlo let out a short laugh. "Find Malvel? You and your friend should go back to Avantia before it is too late. Gorgonia does not welcome foolish heroes."

"We are no fools – we're here to rescue my friend, the wizard Aduro," Tom explained.

"And we're not going back until we find him," Elenna added defiantly.

Kerlo smiled, showing two rows of blackened teeth. "Very well, if you insist..." He stretched

out a hand, pointing across the
marshland with a bony finger. "That
is the best way forwards."

Then dark shadows began to
swirl in front of the lion's gate, and

the mysterious gatekeeper vanished
into thin air.

2

A NEW QUEST

Elenna rubbed her eyes. "He's really gone! Do you think we can believe what he told us?"

Tom shrugged. "I don't know, but it's a start. We have to find Aduro." He stroked Storm. The stallion was trembling, his black coat beaded with sweat. "Everything will be fine," he murmured. He turned to his friend. "Are you ready, Elenna?"

"As ready as I'll ever be," she replied, "although this isn't going to be easy."

"I know, but don't forget that I now have the Golden Armour," Tom said, looking down at the precious relic he was wearing. "The powers it gives me will help us if we have to face Malvel."

As the words left his lips, a flickering light rose from the ground, enclosing Tom in a pale blue glow.

"What's happening?" he shouted.

He tried to punch his way out of the blue forcefield but it would not release him. He felt his armour begin to vibrate. Each piece was shaking itself free of his body.

Elenna threw herself forwards to help, but as her outstretched hands touched the blue glow she was thrown away again.

"Stay back!" Tom yelled, as the blue glow became a column of icy flame. He knew that Elenna could not save him from this magic.

When the flames died down, Tom's Golden Armour was gone. He was left standing in his ordinary clothes, grasping the sword and shield that he had carried since the beginning of his first Quest.

"Tom!" Elenna gasped. "Are you all right?"

"I'm fine," Tom replied, staring down at his worn blue tunic. "But the armour's gone." Despair began to creep over him as he realised what he had lost. "What will we do without it?"

Elenna's eyes were wide with dismay. "Is Malvel really powerful enough to steal the armour from your body?"

Before Tom could reply, the air in front of him shimmered, and a figure began to form. Tom raised his sword. If Malvel was coming to finish them off, then both he and Elenna would fight until their last breath.

But it wasn't Malvel. It was Aduro! Tom lowered his sword in confusion. The king's adviser looked as if he were really standing in front of him. *But isn't Aduro*

Malvel's prisoner? Tom thought. He stepped towards the Good Wizard.

"Tom, be careful." Elenna grabbed his arm. "This could be one of Malvel's tricks."

Tom looked hard at Aduro and the wizard smiled at him. Tom suddenly felt as light as air. He knew that smile anywhere! It could not be faked. "Aduro, it really is you!"

Aduro reached for Tom's hand and shook it firmly. "Yes, it is."

Elenna let out a cry of delight and threw her arms around the Good Wizard. "We were afraid we'd never see you again!"

"But how did you escape from Malvel?" Tom asked.

Aduro smiled. "You both freed me."

Tom and Elenna exchanged a puzzled glance.

"How could we?" Tom asked,

mystified. "We only just got here."

"When you recovered all six pieces of the Golden Armour," Aduro explained, "you gave me the strength to get away."

A warm sense of pride flooded through Tom, but it ebbed away almost instantly. "I've lost the armour now. It vanished just before you came."

Aduro smiled. "Don't worry, Tom. The armour has been returned to its rightful place in King Hugo's palace."

Although Tom was relieved to hear that Malvel hadn't stolen the armour again, he was disappointed that he had lost his powers.

"Of course, you still have your

special gifts," Aduro said, almost as if he had read Tom's mind. "They will always be part of you."

Tom wanted to ask more questions but Aduro didn't give him the chance.

"My time here must be short," the wizard went on, "and there are things that I must tell you. Passing through the lion's gate from Avantia to Gorgonia was a test. You had the courage to do that, and now I know that you are both strong enough to face a new Quest."

Excitement tingled through Tom as he realised that more adventures awaited them.

"What is it?" Elenna asked eagerly.

"Malvel has six more Evil Beasts

here in Gorgonia," the good wizard explained. "They must be destroyed before he has the chance to unleash them on Avantia."

Tom felt the cold touch of fear but he drew himself up, gripping his sword. "While there's blood in my veins," he vowed, "I'll protect Avantia."

"So will I," Elenna added. "And we'll have you and your magic on our side this time, Aduro."

The wizard shook his head. "My magic cannot survive here in Malvel's kingdom. I weaken with every moment I spend in Gorgonia. I have no choice but to go to King Hugo's palace – now."

Tom gazed at him in alarm.

Aduro laid his hand reassuringly on Tom's shoulder. "My thoughts will be with you on your Quest," he said. "I will watch you from the palace, and when I have the strength I will appear to you in visions. But I will not be able to stay for long."

Even while he was speaking Tom could see that the wizard was beginning to look haggard and weak. His firm grip on Tom's shoulder grew light.

"Go quickly!" Tom exclaimed.

The wizard raised a hand in farewell. Then in a swirl of robes and a sudden blaze of white light, Aduro passed through the lion's gate, back into Avantia.

Elenna stared out at the desolate landscape. "How are we going to find these new Beasts?" she asked. "There is nothing here except wasteland."

"Kerlo told us to cross the marsh," Tom replied. "But that was when we were looking for Aduro." He gazed across the evil-smelling swamp, remembering how he had sunk into a similar bog when he was pursuing Soltra the Stone Charmer.

"Let's see what my magical compass can tell us," he suggested, pulling it from his pocket. It had been given to him by his long-lost father, Taladon, and had saved his life before.

The compass needle swung wildly for a moment and then came to rest on the word *Destiny*. The needle was pointing straight across the marsh.

"So this is the way to the next Beast," Elenna said, her eyes bright.

"And to our destiny," Tom replied. "Let's go."

3

MALVEL'S PLOT

Tom and Elenna stepped cautiously onto the edge of the marsh, trying to judge whether there was a firm path across. For an instant, Tom felt himself sink, then his feet came to rest on firm ground.

He peered into the distance, looking for a landmark. They would need something to aim for so that they didn't become disorientated.

Relief surged through him as he saw a cluster of buildings on the horizon.

He turned to Elenna. "Even without the golden helmet, I can still see for long distances," he said happily. "I've spotted something!"

Elenna face split into a grin. "What is it?" she asked.

Tom shaded his eyes with one hand against the angry red of the setting sun, and looked out across the marsh again. "It must be a village," he said. "Let's head for it." He sheathed his sword and took Storm by the bridle.

Elenna nodded and looked for Silver. The wolf was darting around excitedly, but came when

Elenna called him to her side. Tom mounted Storm, and Elenna scrambled up behind him. With Silver padding alongside them, they set out into the marsh. Tom guided Storm carefully, avoiding the pools of water that dotted the boggy ground.

They had not gone far when they heard a furious roar from behind them. Tom spun round in the saddle, ready to draw his sword.

Brilliant white light was shining from the distant lion's gate. A second later, a dark figure burst through it and headed for the marsh, in their direction. Tom caught his breath. It was Tagus the Horse-Man, Good Beast and

protector of Avantia, who had
helped them to defeat Trillion the
Three-Headed Lion.

"He must have followed us
through the gate!" Elenna gasped.

Tagus plunged into the marsh.
Tom slid down from Storm and
splashed back through the mud
towards the horse-man, waving his
arms above his head. "No! Stop!
Go back!" he yelled. He knew that
Tagus couldn't understand what he
said, but he hoped that the Beast
would understand his gestures.

But Tagus did not seem able to
stop. He threw his head back and
let out another roar, full of anger
and frustration. He was trying to
dig his hooves into the swampy

ground, but some invisible force was pulling him onwards, deeper into Gorgonia and across the marsh.

"I've got to try to block him," Tom said. "Keep Storm and

Silver out of the way."

Elenna nodded and guided Storm out of Tagus's path. The stallion was skittish but obeyed. Then she called to Silver, who darted to her side.

The horse-man was upon him now, but Tom did not move out of the way. Tagus reared, his forelegs striking at the air, barely missing Tom's head, trying to fight whatever was pulling him on, but his hooves continued to drag through the mud and he was forced further into the marsh.

Tom leapt forwards and tried to grab one of the horse-man's flailing arms, but it was impossible. Tagus's head thrashed to and fro, and he thrust out his arms as if he were trying to defend himself from an unseen enemy. His skin was shiny with sweat and his eyes rolled back in fear. With a last roar of bewilderment and rage, he broke into a gallop.

Tom's hands clenched as he watched Tagus race across the marsh. His hooves threw up showers of mud, but he went on galloping, faster and faster, until he was a speck in the distance.

Tom turned to Elenna. "Are you thinking what I'm thinking?" he asked.

"Something was forcing Tagus into the marsh," she said. "It must be Malvel."

"I wouldn't be surprised." Tom gazed out across the marsh. Tagus was now completely out of sight. He jumped onto Storm's saddle in front of Elenna. "Tagus was heading towards the village. We have to follow him," he said. "Don't you see? There is a second part to our new Quest."

Elenna furrowed her brow. "I don't understand."

Tom gritted his teeth. "Malvel wants to send Evil Beasts into Avantia once more. So he's pulling the Good Beasts into Gorgonia. Without the Good Beasts, Avantia has no defence!"

53

ACROSS THE DEADLY MARSH

Tom urged Storm forwards through the marsh. The stallion tossed his head nervously but kept on moving, picking his way around pools covered in green scum, through reed beds and across tussocks of grass. With every step his legs sank deeper into the swamp.

"This is no use," Elenna said. "The

ground won't bear the weight of Storm carrying us."

"We'll have to get off and walk," Tom replied.

Without Tom and Elenna on his back, Storm could move more easily. Tom led him carefully, trying to find a firm track to follow. Elenna walked on Storm's other side and Silver brought up the rear, mud splattering all over his grey fur.

Tom's feet sank into the marsh and he felt cold water soaking through his boots. Clouds of flies rose into the air as he brushed past reed beds, and the mud he disturbed gave off a foul smell.

Elenna suddenly let out a cry of

alarm as she tripped and ended up knee-deep in mud. "This is taking too long!" she exclaimed. "Malvel could be hurting Tagus while we're stuck here like this."

Tom grabbed her hand and hauled her out. He was afraid she was right, but all they could do was go on. No one else was able to help Tagus. Glancing around, he spotted a line of trees, bordering the marsh,

in the near distance. Their branches were bare except for a few ragged leaves, and their twisted, black shapes were outlined against the stormy red sky.

"Let's head over there and walk along the edge of the marsh," he suggested, pointing to the trees. "The tree roots will make the ground more solid and keep our feet out of the bog."

"All right," Elenna agreed. "We'll certainly be able to move faster."

Tom was glad to lead Storm up a rough slope out of the swamp and towards the trees. Silver raced ahead, then stopped to shake himself vigorously, scattering mud everywhere.

"Hey, stop that!" Elenna laughed. "I'm muddy enough, thank you."

As Tom approached the spinney he saw that it was thicker than it had looked from a distance, with a narrow path in its midst. Though there weren't any leaves on the trees, the branches criss-crossed and shut out the light.

Tom swung himself into Storm's saddle again. "Let's follow that path," he said decisively. "When we get to the other side of the trees we should be able to loop back to the village and avoid the marsh altogether. It is out of our way, but I still think it will be faster then going across this bog."

"Sounds like a plan," Elenna said, as she climbed up onto Storm.

Tom clicked his tongue to urge the horse into the shadow of the trees. But Storm refused to budge. He was trembling and sweating again.

"Come on, boy." Tom flicked the stallion's neck lightly with the reins. "We can't stay here."

Reluctantly Storm began to move. Elenna called to Silver, but the wolf did not come straightaway. Instead, he stood stiff-legged at the edge of the trees. Elenna called again. Silver let out a chilling howl before following them into the forest, his head down and his tail drooping.

It was dark under the trees, with only a few thin beams of blood-red light finding their way through the tangled branches. The path soon

grew narrower and Tom had to guide
Storm carefully to avoid the sharp
thorns on the bushes. Gnarled tree
roots broke through the ground,
waiting to trip them up.

The air was clammy and Tom found
it hard to breathe. "This is going to

be our hardest Quest yet," he said. "But we'll come through – I know we will!"

Storm rolled his eyes and let out a loud neigh, as if he were agreeing.

"Silver hates this place," Elenna said, glancing down at her friend. The wolf was panting, his tongue lolling out. "But at least we're out of that awful marsh!"

Tom was about to reply when he felt something thin and sharp poke at his ribs. He looked down to see that a low branch from one of the trees was prodding him in the side. He pushed it away but the branch immediately thrust forwards again and poked him even harder.

"Hey, that tree just went for me!"

"It can't have," Elenna retorted. "Trees don't move…"

Her voice died away as the sound of creaking and rustling rose from the forest, almost as if the trees were stretching their limbs. Above his head Tom could see branches moving, though there wasn't a breath of wind.

"They're alive!" he exclaimed.

One of the branches swooped down. Elenna ducked. It retreated, but another branch attacked, its fingers raking at Elenna's hair.

"We've got to get out of here," Elenna cried. "These trees want to hurt us!"

5

MALVEL'S MAP

Tom dug his heels hard into Storm's
sides. "Go!" he shouted.

Storm fled along the path through
the forest. Tom bent low over the
horse's neck, with Elenna clinging
on behind. Silver raced along
beside them.

"Come on, boy!" Tom yelled,
patting Storm's neck to encourage
him. "Faster!"

On either side of the path the trees bent over, reaching out with their limbs to snatch and claw at Tom and Elenna, their branches creaking like cruel laughter. Leaning down to his shield, which was fastened on Storm's saddle, Tom rubbed the piece of Tagus's magical horseshoe that was fixed there. The extra speed it would give them might just save their lives.

Storm's hooves became a blur as he thundered down the path. Thick, thorny bushes were closing in all around them and Tom drew his sword. The skills given to him by the golden gauntlets helped him to hack a way through. Out of the corner of his eye, he spotted an ivy

tendril snake out towards him. It
tried to snatch the weapon from his
grasp, but he was ready for it, and
slashed it away.

"Tom! Look!" Elenna cried, pointing over his shoulder.

Tom saw that they were coming to the end of the forest. He pushed Storm even harder and they burst out into the open again, beneath the swirling red sky of Gorgonia.

Gradually he slowed Storm to a walk. Glancing back, he saw the whole of the forest moving, branches lashing around in fury.

"What happened here?" Elenna asked, looking down at the ground.

All around them the earth was churned up. Trees had been uprooted and tossed aside, their roots twisting up in the air.

"The forest has been ripped up," Tom replied. "I don't know why, but it's lucky for us. I thought we'd never make it out of there."

"Where's the village?" Elenna asked. "Can you still see it?"

He gazed around, looking for the landmark. But even with his magical sight he couldn't spot the village he had seen earlier. Just flat land. "I'm not sure where we are," he replied truthfully. "Tearing through that forest has got us completely lost."

"How about Tagus?" Elenna asked anxiously.

"No sign of him, either," Tom said, shaking his head. "I just hope he hasn't been captured by Malvel." He pulled out his father's compass again, but this time the needle swung to and fro without giving a clear reading.

"We'd better keep going," he began.

Just then a sizzling sound interrupted him, and a flash of red lightning struck the ground. Storm reared with a whinny of fear, and Tom had to struggle to get him under control again.

When the horse was quiet, Tom saw that something was lying on the ground where the lightning had struck. Elenna slid down from Storm's back and ran to pick it up.

"Careful!" Tom warned her, dismounting as well.

Elenna handed Tom what looked like a rolled-up piece of parchment.

Tom shuddered as he touched it. It was greasy animal hide.

Holding the parchment at arm's length, Tom slowly unrolled it.

"It's a map!" Elenna exclaimed. "I wonder if it's magical, like the map of Avantia that Aduro gave us?"

Tom examined the map uneasily. The land it showed was unfamiliar, and across the top of it, in spiky black letters, was the word "Gorgonia". He glanced up at the stormy sky. "Did you send this, Malvel?" he shouted. "Do you think we're going to trust it?"

A familiar cruel laugh rang out. It was Malvel, though there was no sign of the evil wizard.

"We'll rescue Tagus!" Tom vowed defiantly. "And we don't need your map!"

"Ah, but I think you'll find it most useful," Malvel whispered, and then he laughed again, the sound fading on the wind. He was gone.

Tom and Elenna looked down at

the map.

"Look, here's the lion's gate into Avantia." Elenna pointed. "That means we're in the southwest. And there's the forest, and here's the marsh."

Tom traced a line from the forest. "The village is not far from here," he said. "And look – there's a picture of Tagus next to it."

The tiny image of the horse-man suddenly became animated, rearing up and stamping his hooves. His head and upper body thrashed to and fro, as if he were trying to throw off invisible chains.

"Then that's where we must go to help Tagus," Elenna said. "Unless you think the map is trying to trick us."

"I don't completely trust it," Tom declared. "But it's all we've got, so we'll have to take a chance. If Malvel is leading us into a trap, we'll be ready."

He had begun to roll the map up again when Elenna grabbed his hand to stop him. "Look! It's changing!"

Tom stared. Elenna was right. The edges of the forest and marsh were shifting; a tall and jagged rockface appeared, and a waterfall vanished. But the village stayed in the same place. All the landmarks were moving!

"Malvel's trying to confuse us," Tom said grimly. "He will try to make it as hard as possible for us to follow this map."

"Still, the map might help us if we're careful how we use it," Elenna said.

"Yes, you're right. Malvel thinks he can play games with us – but he'll find out he's mistaken. Let's get going."

Tom rolled up the map and stowed it away in Storm's saddlebag. As he and Elenna climbed into the saddle again, a purple moon appeared over the trees, shedding a threatening light over the ruined forest.

Tom urged Storm forwards. He felt Elenna grip his waist and knew that his friend was as determined

as he was. He clenched his hands on the reins.

"Whatever the danger, we'll face it," he said, "for the sake of Avantia."

TROUBLE IN THE VILLAGE

The blood-red sun of Gorgonia was rising again as Tom guided Storm along the rutted road that led into the village.

"At last!" Tom yawned. He was tired after travelling all night. "Maybe we can rest for a bit here and get something to eat."

"I don't know," Elenna replied

doubtfully. "I don't like the look of this place. It's as if no one lives here."

"Maybe they don't," Tom replied, looking round at the crumbling stone houses. Their wooden doors and window shutters were rotting, and most of the windows were dark.

They carried on, passing more derelict houses. After a while they could hear voices ahead. Storm trotted onwards and they came upon a marketplace, set on muddy ground. Ramshackle wooden stalls were laid out in lines, and sellers were shouting out their wares.

"Fresh bread! Get your fresh bread here!"

"Ripe apples! Best ripe apples!"

"Pots to mend? Any pots to mend?"

Tom and Elenna dismounted and led Storm along the first row of stalls, looking at the strange piles of produce heaped up there. The turnips had two prongs, there were mushrooms growing on the apples,

and the carrots were bright blue
with feathery red tops. Everything
was either dried up or worm-eaten.
None of it was fresh.

"Look at this stuff!" Elenna
whispered. "I wouldn't want to eat
any of it."

"Nor would I," Tom agreed,
thinking of the plump apples
and juicy pears that grew in the
orchards of Avantia.

As they walked further into
the market, Tom noticed that the
villagers kept turning to look at
them. A stallholder froze as she
was putting out her goods, sniffed
the air suspiciously, then glared at
them as they went by.

"What's the matter with

everyone?" Elenna asked. "Why are they staring?"

Tom shrugged. "I don't know. Maybe they've never seen a horse as fine as Storm before."

"That doesn't explain why that woman sniffed!" Elenna's voice was indignant. "Does she think we smell bad?"

The woman wasn't the only one, Tom realised. Several of the villagers were sniffing now, as if they were picking up a strange odour.

"We can't smell worse than anything else in this place," Tom declared. "Just ignore them."

A large bearded man suddenly barged into Tom's shoulder,

making him stumble.

"I'm sorry, I–" the man began. Then he broke off, coughing and choking.

Tom tried to pat him on the back, but the man slapped his hand away.

"Don't touch me!" he yelled. "You have the stench of Avantia on you! You're vermin...you're a plague!"

Letting out a roar of rage, he launched himself straight at Tom. But Tom ducked beneath the bearded man's meaty hands and skipped out of the way.

At once, the other people in the marketplace sprang forwards, shouting and cursing. Their faces were twisted with hatred. An old woman waved her stick at Tom and

Elenna. "You've got no right to be here!" she croaked.

"Grab them!" someone else yelled.

They rushed forwards, but halted as Tom drew his sword and swung it round in a circle.

"Keep back," he warned. To Elenna he added, "Get on Storm!"

Elenna jumped nimbly onto the stallion's back. Tom was right behind her but once more the bearded man leapt at him and tried to tackle him to the ground. Again Tom was too quick and neatly side-stepped him. The man ended up face-down in the mud.

Elenna had already set Storm into a trot and Tom jumped up behind her.

"Go, Storm!" Elenna cried.

The stallion sprang forwards into a gallop, hooves pounding through the mud of the street while Silver bounded alongside, yelping in excitement.

Tom looked back over his shoulder. Several market-sellers were running down the road in pursuit. But Storm was too fast for them. They dropped back and the sound of their shouting died away, as Tom and his friends left the last houses of the village far behind.

They'd escaped!

7

A TRAIL
OF BLOOD

At last Elenna drew Storm to a
stop. The ground was covered with
dead yellow grass, and sloped
down into a valley. A sluggish river
wound its way along the bottom,
with a few straggling bushes
growing on the banks.

Tom looked back. There was no
sign that anyone had followed them

from the village. "I think we're safe," he said. "But how are we going to find Tagus? The map told us he was in the village, but they'll attack us if we go back there."

"Let's look at the map again," Elenna suggested, sliding to the ground.

Tom dismounted, pulled Malvel's map out of the saddlebag and unrolled it, trying to ignore its slimy touch. The small figure of Tagus still stood beside the picture of the village.

"The map might be wrong," Elenna said.

Tom nodded. "Or maybe Malvel deliberately lied to us. Perhaps he wanted to lure us to the village because he knew the villagers would hate us."

Elenna pulled her shawl tightly around her shoulders. "We were lucky to get away."

Tom knew she was right. But now there was nothing to tell them where to go next.

"Hey, what's that?" Elenna interrupted his thoughts.

"What?" Tom asked.

"Over there on the grass. It looks like a trail," Elenna replied, pointing.

Tom looked and saw a dark red smear on the yellow grass, leading away over the crest of a hill. He guided Storm over to it, while Silver raced ahead, sniffing the ground. The wolf let out a small whimper.

Tom examined the dark stains. He didn't need Silver's nose to tell him that it was drying blood. Then he felt his shield softly vibrating on Storm's saddle, and saw that the piece of Tagus's horseshoe was glowing faintly!

"Oh, no!" Elenna exclaimed. "It can't be!"

"I think it is," Tom replied, his stomach in knots. "This blood must have come from Tagus."

Still leading Storm, Tom and Elenna followed the trail of blood. It led over the hill and along the top of the valley. Nothing grew there. They were trekking through a barren wasteland.

"There's something ahead," Tom said eventually, peering forwards. His keen sight showed him a twisted tree and Tagus, their friend, lying among the gnarled roots. The horse-man was moaning in pain, and seemed to be straining against something that tethered him to the tree.

"It's Tagus – he's hurt!" Tom said urgently.

They hurried forwards.

Tagus must have heard their approach. He turned his head as Tom and Elenna came up, his eyes filled with pain.

"Oh, look! Tom, that's horrible!" Elenna pointed at one of Tagus's

hind legs. It was caught in the jaws
of a vicious trap, and blood was
still seeping from the wound. A
thick chain tethered the trap to a
root of the tree.

Tom clenched his fists angrily.
"We're going to get you out

of here," he told the Good Beast, wishing the horse-man could understand.

Tom's presence must have soothed Tagus, because he stopped struggling and lay back against the tree roots with a shuddering sigh.

Elenna bent over the trap. "There's something written here. It says 'Torgor'." Puzzled, she looked up at Tom. "What do you think that means?"

"It must be the name of the next Beast we have to face."

Elenna's face screwed up with disgust. "What evil is this? How can one Beast treat another so badly?"

"This is one of Malvel's Beasts," Tom reminded her. "They're all evil to the core."

"Can you get Tagus out of the trap?" Elenna asked.

"I'll try. Lend me your shawl, Elenna."

She gave it to him and Tom wrapped his hands in it, trying to prise open the jaws of the trap. It was no use. The trap would not budge. Drawing his sword, he hacked at the chain, but the blade didn't even scratch the metal.

Tom let out a shout of frustration. "It's too strong!"

"We've got to do something!" Elenna said, looking down at the limp form of the horse-man. "We can't leave him like this."

Tom resheathed his sword. "I can

only see one option: we have to find Torgor and force him to free Tagus."

"Where should we start looking?" Elenna asked.

Tom gazed out at the horizon, searching for an answer. A little way off Silver was sniffing at something in the grass; he looked up at Tom and let out an inviting whine.

"What have you got there, boy?" Tom asked.

He walked across to Silver. There in the grass was a faint set of bloodstained footprints, leading down into the valley.

"Look what Silver's found!" Tom called to Elenna, who had knelt down and was gently stroking

Tagus's head. She jumped up and
came to join him. "Torgor must
have stepped in Tagus's blood."

"Another trail! We can follow it!"
Elenna exclaimed.

Tom shook his head, his hand
going to the hilt of his sword. "I'll
follow Torgor. You should stay
here and look after Tagus. Silver
and Storm can stay with you,

too. They'll help to protect you if Malvel shows up."

"I don't think so." Elenna pointed to Silver, who was waving his tail wildly, waiting for Tom to follow. "He's made up his mind to go with you. Look after him, won't you?"

"Don't worry, I will." Tom went back to Storm and unfastened his shield from the saddle.

Elenna sat down beside Tagus, putting a comforting arm around his shoulders, and waved goodbye to Tom. Part of him wished that she was coming, too; Elenna was a great friend to have in a tight spot. But he shook off this thought. Tagus needed someone to take care of him.

Torgor, you won't escape me, Tom thought, as he strode forwards, his eyes fixed on the trail of blood. *I'm coming to get you!*

1

FACING THE MINOTAUR

The trail led towards the river. Even though Tom was no longer wearing the golden chainmail, he was grateful for the strength of heart it gave him now. He gripped his sword and shield tightly as he braced himself to meet the Beast and stayed alert for any unexpected sounds, but all he could hear was the wind sweeping across the barren hillside.

The dim light from the red sun made it hard for Tom to see, even with his extra-keen sight. Before long, the bloody footprints petered out, but Silver kept running frantically back and forth, letting out excited yelps as he picked up the scent of the Beast.

However, at the riverbank the wolf seemed to lose the trail. He ran up and down, splashing through the shallow water and whining unhappily.

"What is it, boy?" Tom asked. "Where is the Beast?"

Silver let out a frustrated howl, and Tom guessed that the Beast had crossed the river. The water would have destroyed his scent; there was no way of following him any further.

Tom looked back up the hill to where he could still see the twisted tree and the tiny figures of Elenna and Tagus. How were they going to help the horse-man now?

Suddenly Silver let out a warning yelp. Tom turned round and spotted something flying through the air towards him at an impossible speed. He flung up his shield, just in time to fend off a huge section of tree trunk.

In spite of the strength he had been given when he won the golden breastplate, Tom staggered under the force of the blow. Then his knees buckled and he fell to the ground. The tree trunk thumped into the

mud at the edge of the river.

Tom scrambled up, staring in
disbelief at the enormous missile.
Someone – or something – with
incredible strength had just hurled
it across the river. He gazed to the
other side of the sluggish water,
trying to spot his attacker, but could
see nothing.

"Tom! Tom!"

Tom spun round at the sound of Elenna's voice. Mounted on Storm, his friend was racing down the hillside towards him.

"I saw what happened!" she gasped, jumping down from the horse. "I had to come. If someone is trying to attack you, then we fight together."

"Thanks," Tom said. "I–"

He broke off as Elenna's eyes widened. Twisting round, he saw that a pair of horns had appeared above the crest of a low hill on the other side of the river. They were huge, curved and shining, with wickedly sharp points.

"Torgor," Elenna breathed.

The pair of horns was followed by a bull's head, with eyes that reflected the scarlet of the sky. Below the neck was a man's body covered with thick black hair. He wore a leather belt around his waist and in one hand he carried a giant axe with a golden blade. A red jewel glittered where the axe-head met the handle. Torgor was much taller than Tagus. He let out a roar of fury.

Tom's heart beat faster and his palms sweated as he reached for his sword. The huge Beast strode down the riverbank and waded through the water towards him. Even though Tom knew that he still had the powers of the Golden Armour, he felt helpless in the face

of such a monster.

But he stood his ground. He
wouldn't give in without trying to
fight.

"While there's blood in my veins,"
he vowed, "I'll defeat this Beast."

1

9

BATTLE BEGINS

Torgor raced out of the river and swung his axe above his head.

"Look out!" Tom yelled at Elenna, who was placing an arrow in her bow. As the axe whirled down towards them, Tom and Elenna leapt aside. The golden blade slammed down, shaking the ground so that they both lost their balance and sprawled flat on their backs.

Tom jumped to his feet, slashing at Torgor with his sword. But the Beast barely noticed the blows. Jerking the axe-head out of the ground, he headed up the hill, straight for the tree where Tagus still lay tethered. He swiped his axe through the air as he stalked towards the injured horse-man.

"He's going to kill Tagus!" Elenna gasped. "We've got to stop him!"

Tom launched himself up the hill. He couldn't believe how fast Torgor was. Even with the extra speed given to him by Tagus's horseshoe token, Tom had a hard time keeping up with the Evil Beast's giant strides. He left Elenna and their animal friends far behind, and reached

the hilltop just a few paces behind
Torgor.

The Beast stood over the trapped
horse-man, who was staring up at
his captor with fury in his eyes.
Rage flooded through Tom. As Torgor
raised his weapon, Tom dropped
his sword and shield, leapt up and

caught the axe by the blade. The Beast let out a bellow of fury and waved the axe wildly, but Tom managed to cling on, even though the golden blade cut into his palms.

As Torgor whirled the axe through the air, Tom felt his hands slipping. He lost his grip on the axe-head and was thrown to the ground. The fall knocked the breath out of him. Gasping, he forced himself up onto his hands and knees. He could feel the hope in his heart failing. He just didn't have the strength to combat this Beast.

A short laugh made him look up. To his astonishment, Kerlo the gatekeeper was standing in front of him, shaking his head.

"You're just like your father, Taladon," Kerlo said. "Too stubborn to admit defeat."

Tom's fury surged up again. "Leave me alone!" he shouted. What right did Kerlo have to criticise him or his father? Anger and determination gave him the strength to stand, and he grabbed his sword and shield to attack the Beast once more.

An approving smile spread across Kerlo's features, and Tom realised that the gatekeeper had been deliberately trying to anger him so that he would get up and fight again. Was Kerlo on their side after all?

Tom started towards Torgor. But he heard a furious yelping and turned to see that Elenna was at the top of the hill with Silver and Storm. His friend was busy firing arrow after arrow at the Beast's back, but they bounced off his thick hide. Tom swung his sword around his head and jumped forwards to hack at the Beast's muscular legs. But Torgor easily kicked the blade aside.

Tagus tried to back away from the minotaur. But the horse-man's struggles only drove the teeth of the trap further into his flesh and a new stream of blood began to trickle down to his hooves. He kicked out with his forelegs, but the Evil Beast was out of his reach.

Brave Tagus can't fight like this, Tom thought. *If only we could free him!*

As Torgor raised the axe above his head once more, Tom had an idea. He sprang between the two Beasts, just in front of the chain that tethered Tagus to the tree, and swung his sword at Torgor.

The minotaur let out a bellow of rage and swung the axe down with all his might towards Tom. At the last moment, Tom dived to one side. He felt his hair ruffle in the blade's slipstream and heard a loud clang as it struck the chain.

The links had parted. The chain was broken!

Tagus let out a roar. Rolling over, Tom saw him leap up, his hooves pawing the ground. Still trailing the vicious trap from one leg, he threw

himself upon Torgor. As the two
Beasts wrestled together, Tom felt a
stab of pride. How brave the horse-
man was! He surged forwards to
help, and rained blows onto Torgor's
back. Silver darted in and out,
nipping at Torgor's ankles.

"Tagus, you can do it!" Elenna cried.

The two Beasts churned the ground as they fought. Torgor wrapped his arms around Tagus's body, trying to crush the life out of him, and lowered his head to gore the horse-man with his horns. As quick as lightning, Tagus reached up, grabbed the nearest horn and twisted it.

A drawn-out cry of agony came from Torgor as Tagus wrenched the horn away from his head. The minotaur instantly let go of the horse-man, who dropped to the ground, panting. Torgor stumbled backwards, then grew suddenly still.

"That's it!" Tom cried. Hope flooded through him. "Torgor's strength is in his horns. That's the way to defeat him!"

10

BATTLE ENDS

Tom raised his sword to attack
Torgor, but before the blow could
fall, the Beast sprang into action
again. He tossed his injured head
and rushed at Tagus with a bellow
of rage.

"Elenna!" Tom hissed. "Keep
Torgor busy! Make sure he doesn't
notice me!"

Elenna dashed forwards and

fired more arrows at the Beast,
this time aiming for his face. The
arrows seemed to sting Torgor like
irritating flies; he batted at them
and swung his head round to fix his
red eyes directly on Elenna.

Tom dropped his shield but kept a
grip on his sword as he climbed the
tree. He worked his way along one
of the branches until he was almost

directly above Torgor.

With a loud battle-cry that echoed across the deserted land, Tom leapt down from the tree and swung his sword at Torgor's remaining horn. The blade sliced right through it and the Beast froze with his axe raised just above Elenna's head. The red jewel set in the axe-head flared with sudden light and fell to the ground.

Tom landed lightly beside it and picked it up. His hands were still bleeding from clinging onto the axe's golden blade. He hadn't been aware of the pain until now.

"Tom!" Elenna gasped. "Look at Torgor!"

Tom straightened up. Red light

surrounded Torgor, gradually
hardening until it encased the
Beast in a ruby prison. It reminded
Tom of an insect trapped in amber.
The Beast's mouth was still open
in a roar of fury, but no sound
came out.

"You did it, Tom!" Elenna
exclaimed. "You defeated Torgor."

With a long gasp of relief Tom
knelt beside his shield and touched
his wounded hands to another of
his magical tokens: the talon of
Epos the Flame Bird. At once the
blood on his hands disappeared
and the wounds closed up, leaving
no scars.

At the same moment, Tom realised
that somehow the leather belt

Torgor had worn was now wound around his own waist. Six slots were positioned along its length, and it seemed right for Tom to place the red jewel in the first of these.

"I wonder if this will give me another power, like the tokens in my shield and the pieces of Golden Armour," he said thoughtfully.

"Can you feel anything?" Elenna asked eagerly.

"No…" Tom began, then broke off as he heard a voice speaking inside his head. The voice was too weak for him to hear distinct words, but he could sense a powerful feeling of gratitude.

Tom looked at Tagus, astonished.

The horse-man nodded.

"That's it!" Tom exclaimed. "Elenna, I know what Tagus is feeling! The red jewel must help me to communicate with the Good Beasts of Avantia."

A huge smile spread over Elenna's face. "That's wonderful!"

"Tagus," Tom asked, "is it true that Malvel has captured all the Good Beasts? Are they all here in Gorgonia?"

Yes. Tagus's voice came through more clearly now.

Pain and anger flooded through Tom, as if the horse-man were showing him what the other Beasts were suffering.

Tom exchanged a glance with

Elenna. "This Quest has only just begun."

Suddenly he became aware of his shadow stretching in front of him. A blue-white light was shining brightly behind him. At the same moment, Elenna exclaimed, "Aduro!"

Tom whirled round to see the Good Wizard standing under the tree. The gnarled trunk was visible through the wizard's body, and Tom realised it was only a vision.

"Well done, Tom," Aduro said. "Well done, both of you." He beckoned to Tagus, who limped towards him, his leg still in the trap.

"I cannot stay long," Wizard

Aduro went on. "I have little strength in this place, and I must use it to send Tagus back to his home in Avantia. Tagus, are you ready?"

The horse-man nodded. Tom heard the word *Farewell* echoing in his mind. "Goodbye, Tagus," he said.

"Good luck!" Elenna called.

Aduro raised his arms and the blue-white light appeared again, flaring up as it transformed into the lion's gate. Through it, Tom could see the green plains of Avantia. A pang of homesickness shot through him, but he realised it would be a long time before he could return.

Tagus hobbled through the gate,

but the moment his hooves touched the green grass of Avantia the trap fell off his leg and he began to gallop. The terrible wound was healed. He raised his hand in a last farewell before racing into the distance.

Then the bright light faded and Aduro was gone.

Tom and Elenna turned to face each other.

"I'm glad we saw that," Elenna said softly. "I needed to know that Tagus was all right."

"Me too," Tom agreed. "Meanwhile, we remain in Malvel's evil kingdom. We've work to do here."

"I can't help wondering where Malvel is," Elenna went on as she began to collect up her spent arrows. "I'm surprised he hasn't turned up."

Tom suppressed a shudder. He didn't want to think about what the evil wizard might be up to.

"Never mind Malvel," he replied. "We have more Beasts to free."

"I wonder which one will be next," Elenna said.

Tom looked around for their animal friends. Storm was waiting a little way down the hill, while Silver had padded up to the ruby prison surrounding Torgor and was sniffing curiously at its base.

Tom recovered his shield and went to tie it onto Storm's saddle. Then he saw that the talon he had received from Epos the Flame Bird was shining and vibrating softly.

"That's it," he said. "The next Beast we have to save is Epos."

He turned and looked out across the barren hills of this strange new kingdom. Somewhere out here, another Good Beast needed help.

Whatever it took, he, Elenna, Storm and Silver would rise to the challenge!

CONGRATULATIONS, YOU HAVE COMPLETED THIS QUEST!

At the end of each chapter you were
awarded a special gold coin.
The QUEST in this book was
worth an amazing 11 coins.

Look at the Beast Quest totem picture
inside the back cover of this book to
see how far you've come in your journey
to become

MASTER OF THE BEASTS.

The more books you read,
the more coins you will collect!

Do you want your own
Beast Quest Totem?

1. Cut out and collect the coin below
2. Go to the Beast Quest website
3. Download and print out your totem
4. Add your coin to the totem
www.beastquest.co.uk/totem

11

Don't miss the next exciting Beast Quest book, SKOR THE WINGED STALLION!

Read on for a sneak peek...

CHAPTER ONE

VISION IN THE WATER

"We have to clean you up," said Elenna.

Tom and his friend stood beside the river that wound through the dusty Gorgonian plains. It was nothing like the clear streams of Avantia. Here the water was brown and sludgy. Every so often, bubbles escaped to the surface, bursting and filling the air with rotten-smelling yellow gas.

Elenna dabbed the gashes on Tom's arm where Torgor the Minotaur's mighty axe had wounded him. The enchanted talon in Tom's shield, given to him by Epos the Flame Bird, had run out of power before it could heal all of his injuries. It had been Tom's toughest fight yet, but he had managed to free Tagus the Horse-Man from the clutches of Torgor. Now the Good Beast was safely back in Avantia, away from

Malvel's evil.

"Do you think the herbs will work?" asked Tom.

Elenna smiled as she ground up the herbs Tom's aunt had given them. Mixed with some water from her flask, they became a thick paste. Silver the wolf watched as she worked the paste into Tom's wounds.

"Thank you," he said. He didn't know how he would have survived without Elenna on his Quests.

The pain in his arm began to ebb away.

"It's working!" he cried.

The memory of the battle would take longer to fade, though. Torgor was more deadly than any Beast they had faced before. If there were other such creatures in Gorgonia, Tom knew he would need all his strength and courage to defeat them.

Elenna was bandaging the last of the linen dressings over Tom's gashes when Silver leaped to his feet and began pacing along the riverbank, barking wildly at the water.

Tom's horse Storm stamped his hooves and shook his mane, then backed away from the river's edge.

"What's got into Storm and Silver?" asked Elenna.

"Something's spooking them," said Tom. He peered into the water. The current seemed to have stopped. Silver let out a high-pitched whine as a ripple appeared in the middle of the water.

The two friends gazed into the river as the patterns there shifted.

Gradually they could make out the lines of a mouth, then a nose, then two eyes. Ripples like long white hairs framed the image. The mouth moved in little waves.

Elenna gasped.

"Aduro!" said Tom.

It was their friend, the Good Wizard of Avantia.

"Greetings, Tom and Elenna," the vision in the water called.

"Greetings," they replied.

"Once again, congratulations on overcoming Torgor," said Aduro.

"Tagus sends his thanks from Avantia."

Elenna squeezed Tom's arm, and Aduro continued.

"But, as you know, my magic is weak here in Gorgonia – the gateway between worlds saps my energy. I don't have the power to stay with you long."

"Tell us, Aduro," said Tom, "what is our next mission?"

"You must track down a new Beast," said Aduro. "Its name is Skor."

Tom shot Elenna a look. She shrugged, looking mystified. Aduro's face began to blur at the edges, and his words became distant. His magic was fading.

"Beware," he whispered. "I give you a final warning: danger will come from both earth and air. Remember, earth and air…"

The face melted back into the water.

"He's gone!" cried Tom.

"What is Skor?" said Elenna. "How can it be a danger by earth and air?"

"I don't know," said Tom, "but we have to find out. We already know that Epos is in danger." After the defeat of Torgor, the flame bird's talon in Tom's shield had begun to glow, calling for their help.

Tom picked up his shield, swung it onto his back, and tightened the magic belt around his waist. One of the belt's slots already contained the red jewel he had captured from Torgor. It gave him the ability to communicate with the Beasts. But there were five slots left to fill. Tom wondered what new powers he would gain on this Quest.

Read
SKOR THE WINGED STALLION
to find out more!